Bear's Winter Party

Deborah Hodge

PICTURES BY
Lisa Cinar

GROUNDWOOD BOOKS   HOUSE OF ANANSI PRESS   TORONTO   BERKELEY

For my family, with love and thanks for all the wonderful parties — in winter and in every season! — DH

For Nico, Poppy and Pancake and all the other wild animals I love. — LC

Text copyright © 2016 by Deborah Hodge
Illustrations copyright © 2016 by Lisa Cinar
Published in Canada and the USA in 2016 by Groundwood Books

Groundwood Books / House of Anansi Press
groundwoodbooks.com

We acknowledge for their financial support of our publishing program the Canada Council for the Arts, the Ontario Arts Council and the Government of Canada.

Library and Archives Canada Cataloguing in Publication
Hodge, Deborah, author
Bear's winter party / Deborah Hodge ; pictures by Lisa Cinar.
Issued in print and electronic formats.
ISBN 978-1-55498-853-2 (bound).—ISBN 978-1-55498-854-9 (pdf)
I. Cinar, Lisa, illustrator II. Title.
PS8565.O295B42 2016   jC813'.6   C2015-908345-1
C2015-908346-X

The illustrations were done in watercolor and colored pencil, with finishing touches added in Photoshop and magic spells.
Design by Michael Solomon
Printed and bound in Malaysia

Canada Council for the Arts
Conseil des Arts du Canada

ONTARIO ARTS COUNCIL
CONSEIL DES ARTS DE L'ONTARIO
an Ontario government agency
un organisme du gouvernement de l'Ontario

With the participation of the Government of Canada
Avec la participation du gouvernement du Canada

Canadä

FSC
www.fsc.org
MIX
Paper from responsible sources
FSC® C012700

BEAR LIVED in a forest on the side of a mountain. He felt at home among the trees. He nibbled on sweet wild berries. He sipped cool water from the stream. He breathed in the fresh mountain air.

Bear loved living in the forest, but sometimes he got lonely.
When Bear picked berries, Deer ran and hid deep in the woods.
When Bear fished in the stream, Beaver slapped his tail and dove underwater. When Bear collected hazelnuts and honey, Chickadee flew to the top of the tallest tree. Squirrel scurried into her nest, Hare hopped away, and Fox slipped into his burrow.

Wherever he went, Bear heard the other animals talking about him.

"He's so big!" said Squirrel.

"His claws are long," said Hare.

"His teeth are sharp," said Deer.

"His voice makes a rumbling sound," said Chickadee.

Bear spent the summer by himself. In the fall, he was still alone.

"I wish I had a friend," he said.

Bear saw that the days were growing short and the air was getting chilly. It was almost time for his long winter sleep.

"I need to do something now!" he said.

Bear got to work. He made invitations. "Come to my Winter Party," they said.

Then he delivered them — one for Deer deep in the woods, one for Beaver near the stream, one for Fox at his burrow and another for Chickadee high up in a tree. He left the last ones for Hare and Squirrel outside their homes.

Bear hurried back to his den. He swept the floor. He hung an evergreen bough on his front door. He decorated his walls with sprigs of holly and bright red berries. He roasted hazelnuts and made trays of huckleberry tarts and honey-ginger cookies. Then he lit a fire in the fireplace and set a lantern in the window. Last of all, he brewed a big pot of spiced cranberry tea. He was ready!

Bear looked out the window. He saw that snowflakes were falling and the afternoon was growing dark.

"No one is coming," he said sadly.

When he had almost given up hope, Bear saw Deer peeking out from behind a tree. With him were Beaver and Fox. Chickadee, Hare and Squirrel were there, too.

"What will they do?" Bear wondered.

Chickadee was brave. She flew to the window of Bear's den. She peeked in and saw how warm and beautiful it was.

"Let's go in," she called to the others.

Slowly, very slowly, the animals crept closer to the den. When they finally got to the door, Beaver knocked — just a tiny knock.

"We're here for the party," he said in a small voice.

"Come in," said Bear. "I am so glad to meet you!"

All the animals squeezed inside.
Bear passed around bowls
of roasted hazelnuts and plates
of honey-ginger cookies and
huckleberry tarts. He poured cups of
spiced cranberry tea.

"Would anyone like seconds?" he
asked.

At first the animals were quiet, but one by one they began to talk.

"These nuts are delicious," said Squirrel.

"May I have another cup of tea?" asked Hare.

Fox said, "I didn't know bears could bake."

Bear smiled. "I love to bake," he said. "Would you like another cookie?"

After the animals finished their tea and treats, Chickadee suggested they have a sing-along.

"I'll start," she said, "and you can join in."

Soon all the animals were singing and tapping their feet. Beaver tapped his tail. Bear clapped his paws in time with the music. Then Fox pulled out his harmonica and began to play. Bear did a little jig in the middle of the room. Everyone cheered!

"Would anyone like to dance with me?" asked Bear.

Before long, the whole group was dancing. Round and round the den they went, swinging and swaying, whirling and twirling, bobbing and bouncing.

"This is so much fun!" said Hare.

"I could dance forever," said Bear.

After many songs, the music slowed down and the dancing stopped. Bear saw that the lantern was burning low and the fire was almost out. He knew his party was ending.

As the animals got ready to leave, Bear said, "Thank you for coming. I hope you had a good time." Then he gave them each a gift — a jar of his own blackberry jam, tied with a ribbon. "I made it myself," he said.

"That was a great party," said Fox.
"Thank you for inviting me," said Deer.
"I'd like to come back," said Beaver.
"Sleep well," said Squirrel.
"See you in the spring," said Hare.

Bear gave each one of them a big furry hug.
"Come again," he said.
Chickadee kissed Bear on his cheek.
"You are a good friend," she said.
The animals wandered through the trees back
to their own homes. Bear heard them humming as
they went.

He looked out the window. The snow was falling quickly now. Soon the whole forest would be covered in a thick blanket of white.

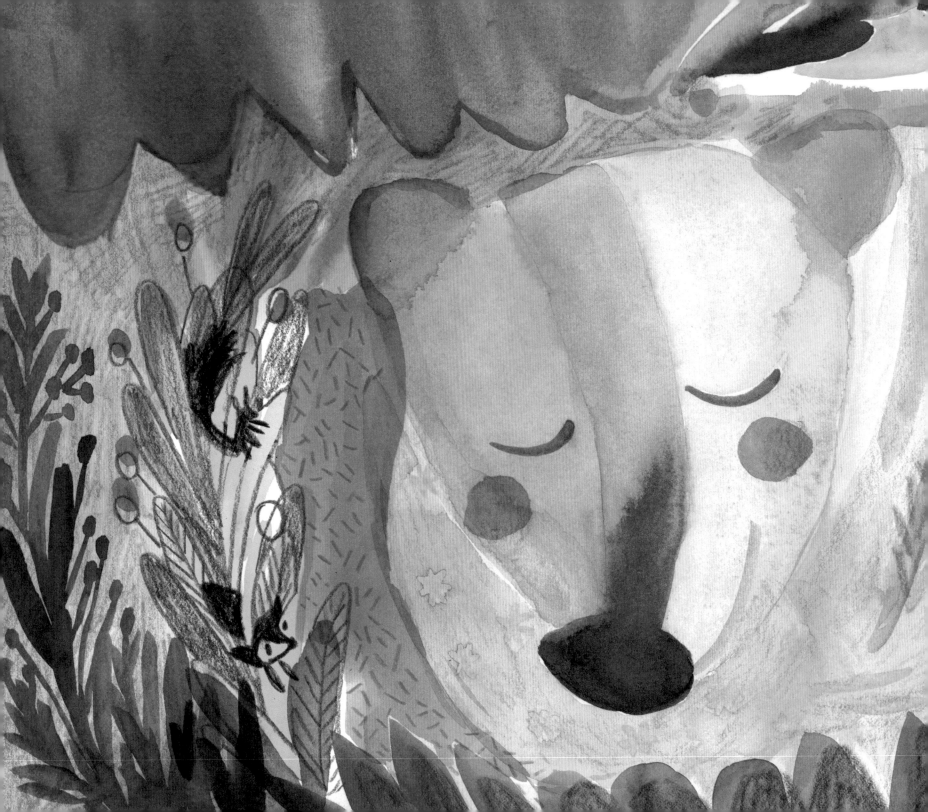

Bear put the dishes in the sink. He blew out
the lantern and climbed into his bed.

"It's time to go to sleep," he said with a yawn.

He pulled the quilt up to his chin and closed
his eyes. As he drifted off, he gave a happy sigh.

For Bear knew that when spring came and he
woke up, he would have a forest full of friends.

BEAR'S HONEY-GINGER COOKIES

Bear loves to bake, and he'd like to share his recipe with you. Maybe you will have a winter party, too! Find your favorite cookie cutters to make your own delicious honey-ginger cookies.

In a mixing bowl, using a hand mixer, cream together:
- ½ cup softened butter
- ½ cup granulated sugar

Beat into the creamed mixture:
- 1 egg
- ¼ cup honey
- ¼ cup molasses
- 1½ tsp vinegar

In another bowl, stir together:
- 2½ cups flour
- 1½ tsp ground ginger
- ½ tsp ground cinnamon
- ½ tsp ground cloves
- 1 tsp baking powder
- ½ tsp baking soda
- pinch of salt

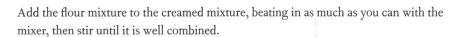

Add the flour mixture to the creamed mixture, beating in as much as you can with the mixer, then stir until it is well combined.

With your hands, form the dough into a ball.

Roll the dough ¼ inch thick on a lightly floured surface. Use your cookie cutters to make cutouts, then place them about 1 inch apart on a greased cookie sheet.

If you like, decorate the unbaked cookies with colorful candies, sprinkles, raisins or chocolate chips.

Bake at 350°F for 8 to 10 minutes, or until cookies are firm around the edges. (Ask for an adult's help.)

Cool slightly, then enjoy! Makes about 2 dozen.